In this story, Finn the leprechaun is challenged by Dinny, whose greed is second to none ...

Look out for other

TALL TALES

Catherine O'Neil is a retired teacher living in upstate New York. She has an MA in art, specifically printmaking, and is a skilled illustrator. She returned to the USA in 1988, after several years in Europe, and retired from teaching in July 1999. Two years ago she began to write for children. Today she continues writing and lives on a country road, sharing her home with her two British cats, Sandy and Honey. Catherine O'Neil is also the author of *The Leprechaun's Challenge*, another tall tale about Finn the Leprechaun.

Dedicated to those in my life who encouraged me to follow my dream – Dee Robbins, Paul A Grizzelle-Reid SCJ, George O'Connell and Jim McSweeney.

Catherine O'Neil

Illustrations: Mass

THE O'BRIEN PRESS

DUBLIN

First published 2002 by The O'Brien Press Ltd,
20 Victoria Road, Dublin 6, Ireland.
Tel. +353 1 4923333; Fax. +353 1 4922777
E-mail: books@obrien.ie
Website: www.obrien.ie

ISBN: 0-86278-733-5

British Library Cataloguing-in-Publication Data
A catalogue record for this title is available from the British Library

1 2 3 4 5 6
02 03 04 05 06

The O'Brien Press receives
assistance from

The Arts Council
An Chomhairle Ealaíon

Editing, layout and design: The O'Brien Press Ltd
Illustrations: Mass
Cover separations: C&A Print Services
Printing: The Guernsey Press Co. Ltd

Contents

Chapter 1:
Dinny and Katie

Dinny O'Shaughnessy was the laziest man in all of County Mayo, and the laziest by far in Castlebar, where he lived.

His favourite sport was wrestling the bed linens. His mother always told him, 'Dinny, lad, you've got dropsy and heart trouble!' When he asked, 'What do you mean, Mammy?' she would reply, 'You drop into your bed, and haven't the heart to get out!'

She worried. She fretted. It changed Dinny not a bit. He would simply yawn, sigh and turn over in his bed.

At the ripe old age of eighteen, Dinny roused himself just long enough to ask for the hand of 'Katie darlin'', the only daughter of Sheila and Conn Donnahey. Conn, now a widower, lived in a snug, cosy cottage a little way down the glen. Katie was a hard worker. As a schoolgirl, she had won first prize for spelling at the village school.

The villagers were stunned when she agreed to wed him.

'What is a clever girl like Katie doing wedding a lout like Dinny O'Shaughnessy?' bellowed Deaf Peter down at the Shamrock Arms, the village pub.

'It'll be the end of poor Katie. She'll be slavin' her life long,' screeched Mad Maura Connolly over her backyard fence.

''Tis a blessed thing that my poor Sheila has gone to her reward, God rest her soul!'

muttered Conn Donnahey, as he tended his sheep on the hills. ''Tis a sad, sad day we've come to that my only daughter marries the likes of Dinny O'Shaughnessy. No good will come of it!'

Dinny's mum knew otherwise. He had lived with her his whole life long, and she knew that his wit could lighten the darkest of days. Not a single day went by that he didn't tickle her funny bone with a joke or a riddle that was making the rounds in the pub. She knew, too, that Dinny was a great lover. He loved his family more than life itself. He might not be the most ambitious lad, but he would make a good husband.

Besides, it was love, and there was no stopping it. On a clear summer's day, all the villagers of Castlebar turned out to wish them well, as Katie darlin' Donnahey and Dinny

O'Shaughnessy pledged their life and their love to each other in the parish church of Saint Brendan. It may have been a sign of things to come that Dinny was late for the service, that he yawned halfway through the marriage vows, and that he had forgotten to buy a ring for his bride.

They moved into the Donnahey cottage with Katie's father.

Conn Donnahey gave his son-in-law five sheep as a wedding present, and agreed to share grazing rights on his land with the lad. Dinny discovered that he loved tending sheep. He could lay out under the trees all day, chewing on a blade of grass, and doze to his heart's content.

Katie gave birth to five children in their first five years together. Three of them were boys, and Katie named them Michael,

Shamie and Jeremiah (Dinny found that trying to think of names was too much like work, so he left it to his wife). The other two children were girls of course, and Katie named them Rosaleen and Mary Kate. As they grew, the boys took after their father, loving nothing better than to lounge around all day. The girls were images of their mother, keeping the cottage clean and neat, keeping the family's clothes washed and pressed, and tending the garden in season.

Although she loved her family dearly, Katie was tired out. She was weary and looked twenty times her age.

'Kick him out, a stór,' her father would urge her. 'The cottage will be yours when I pass. There's no future with him. He's a do-nothing. Look at the lads. They will grow to be just like him. Is that what you want, daughter of mine? Your sainted mother, Lord have mercy on her soul, would be turning in her grave if she could see you now.'

'But I love him, Da, and he loves me,' was all Katie would answer, and nobody can argue with love.

Time drifted by slowly. The children grew bigger and hungrier, Katie grew more exhausted and Dinny, if anything, grew ever more lazy. Nothing changed, and it seemed that nothing ever would.

Chapter 2:
Dinny's Luck is Made

One fine summer's day, with the sun shining brightly, the grass sparkling green in the dew of the morning and the sheep grazing contentedly, Dinny was lying half awake, stretched out on a particularly comfortable patch of grass, with the sheep all around him. He was watching a butterfly fluttering through the air, when he heard a 'tap, tap, tap,' sound, like someone rapping at a door.

'What could that be?' he wondered to himself. He lay there for a long time listening, hoping that he wouldn't have to investigate.

'Ah, well,' he said to himself at last, 'I suppose I'd best be havin' a look.'

With great effort, Dinny stretched out his long legs, flexed his arms and sat up. He began to poke about here and there, hither and yon, in the surrounding gorse and heather. He was just about to wake his fine strapping sons, who were fast asleep in a heap nearby, when he spied a tiny motion in a gorse bush just in front of him. He froze.

'Holy Mother of God!' he said to himself, pulling the branches carefully aside. 'A leprechaun, patchin' some shoes. 'Tis my lucky day indeed. If I can catch hold of him before he spies me, his gold will be mine, and I'll never have to work a day in my life.'

Dinny looked around furtively. He needed something to use for a trap. A skilled leprechaun hunter he was not. He thought

about getting his sons to help, but he knew that if he woke them, the noise and confusion would scare off the wee creature. It would be gone in a second, never more to be seen in these parts. He would only have one chance.

Dinny O'Shaughnessy was not without resources. Hadn't he won the heart of the cleverest girl in all of County Mayo, Katie darlin' Donnahey? He thought hard and quickly, fearing the fairy shoemaker might notice him at any moment and disappear. Dinny silently took the cap off his head and, in the blink of an eye, scooped the leprechaun up in it. Then he reached in and pulled him out by the scruff of the neck.

'Mike, Jerry, Shay,' he shouted (he never could be bothered with saying their whole names). 'Get yourselves up, and give me a hand here. Our luck is made this day!'

The three lads slowly stirred and rubbed the sleep out of their eyes. When they spied their da holding the wiggling and wriggling imp, for the first time in their short lives they came a-running. Dinny gave out instructions:

'Mike, go get your ma, and tell her to bring a sack. I've got me a leprechaun here. He's struggling something fierce, so I won't be able to hold out for long. Hurry, lad.'

'Jer, you get yourself to Paddy Gallagher the handyman and tell him you need a pen for one of the lambs. Don't tell him why. If he asks, you could hint one of them is ailin'. We don't want the whole village to know what we're about.

'Shay, you keep watch on yonder pathway. Hide in the bushes. We must keep this a secret for a while. If someone comes along the roadway, give a hoot or a whistle.'

It is well known in Ireland that to capture a leprechaun can make a man wealthy, wealthier than the ancient kings. It is also well known that leprechauns do not take well to being captured. They will try by struggling, fighting, and finally trickery, to escape their captors.

'Ugh, ach, I can't breathe, ye big dolt,' sputtered the leprechaun. 'You're cuttin' off me wind!'

'Don't be tryin' none of that leprechaun foolery on me,' scoffed Dinny. 'I've heard tell of all your tricks. You've made me day. I'll not work ever again!'

'Aye, you're a lazy lump,' spat the leprechaun. 'I've seen ye here in the fields, day in and day out. Ye don't work anyway!'

Dinny's face was getting redder and redder, and his temper was ready to burst. Just as he was about to take one hand off the leprechaun's neck and bop him over the head, it dawned on him what was happening.

'You'll not be trickin' me! Say what you will. I'll keep me hands in place until me darlin' Katie brings a sack. Then we'll have you good and proper.'

Back in the village, Katie darlin' was beside herself. When her lad Michael brought the news, she thought her menfolk had gone out of their heads altogether. Nevertheless, she dumped the potatoes out of a sack, and hurried off with it to find out what possessed her husband. She arrived just in time to hear Dinny and the leprechaun yelling at each other.

'By Saint Brigid and all the saints in heaven, Dinny, 'tis true. You've got yourself a leprechaun, or are me eyes playin' tricks on me?'

'Hurry, Katie darlin', I can scarce hold on any longer.'

A quick flick of the wrist and Katie had the sack around the leprechaun. She tied the top of it in a tight knot. Katie looked at Dinny. Dinny looked at Katie. And right there, in the fields above Castlebar, they danced a little jig.

Chapter 3:
The Riddle

When they arrived home, arm in arm and singing at the tops of their voices, Jeremiah had a makeshift cage awaiting them in front of the cottage. The furious little fairy man was dumped unceremoniously into it.

When the dust had settled and dusk was creeping over the day, they brought the cage into the cottage. Katie and Dinny pulled up a chair on either side of it. Old Conn Donnahey was sat by the fire, smoking his clay pipe and warming his bones. The children were falling all over each other to get a peek.

'Quiet down, quiet down, the lot of you.' ordered Dinny.

'I'll not be havin' anything to do with this,' muttered Conn from his place near the hearth. 'A fool you are if you think you can get something for nothin'. Look at the poor thing all caged up. You'll be bringin' a spell of bad luck over the household, Dinny O'Shaughnessy. Except for the fact that Katie darlin' loves you beyond all reason, I'd have had you out of this house long ago.'

'Hush your mouth, old man,' said Dinny. 'Sure, Katie is in on this too.'

'Is that true, daughter?' asked Conn.

'The truth is, I'm havin' mixed feelins about it, Dinny,' spoke up Katie. 'Of course, I'd like the gold too, but isn't our real fortune all around us – our family and our home? Seein' the creature trapped in that pen bothers me more than a little. I'm thinkin' maybe Da is right.'

Ignoring Katie's words, Dinny turned to the cage, and asked, 'Have you a name, leprechaun?'

'Sure and I do. I am Finn, maker of shoes, and servant of King Finbar, king of all the fairies in Ireland. He'll not be happy when he hears of this, lummox!'

'Well, we have you now, Finn, me lad. According to fairy law, you must reveal where you keep your gold, and turn it over to us,' Dinny told him.

'Aye, that I know. However, ye must answer me riddle first. If ye can solve it in two days' time, the gold is yours. If not, ye must release me, or King Finbar will send all his fairy warriors to destroy your whole household.'

'A riddle? Did you hear that, my Katie? Finn here doesn't know I married the smartest girl in all of County Mayo. All right, Finn, maker of shoes, tell us the riddle.'

'Here it is then: What is greater than God, and more evil than the devil? The poor have it. The rich need it. If ye eat it ye will die.'

'That's a riddle, to be sure.' laughed Dinny. 'Tell him the answer, Katie. We'll be rich before the sun rises in the eastern sky tomorrow.'

Katie looked at Dinny. Dinny looked at Katie. Her eyes were wide and she was wearing a stunned expression. 'Dinny, what has come over ye? Ye can't put the whole burden on me. I can think of nothing. Give me some time, a ghrá. And do some thinkin' yourself.'

Finn glared at Katie from his small cell. 'What is your answer, woman of the house?

Ye must tell me in no uncertain terms. Ye must say, "My answer is ..."'

Dinny looked around at his family. They all stared back, dumbfounded, except for Conn, who gave a chuckle, tamped out his pipe and roused himself from his seat by the fire. "Tis off to bed I'm goin'. Get you off too. Morning comes soon and there is work to be done. 'Tis clear there's no fortune on the table this night.'

'Cover the cage with a tea towel, Dinny, and give Finn a rest. Off with the rest of you. We'll solve this puzzle in the morning.' Katie ordered.

Chapter 4:
THE SEARCH FOR THE ANSWER

The sun rose brilliantly over the green hills of County Mayo the next morning. A light heart shone even more brightly in each member of the O'Shaughnessy family, as they piled in for their breakfast, sleepy-eyed and tumbling over each other. Katie darlin' stirred the porridge on the stove. Dinny stirred the fire.

'Is he still here, Da, or did Finn the leprechaun disappear in the night?' asked little Rosaleen, wiping the sandman's grains from her eyes.

‘I’m still here,’ came a grumpy voice from the covered cage. ‘I could use a cup of tea and some stirabout. Would ye have me starve to death?’

Katie served Finn a small portion of their fare, carefully lifting the cage door just a fraction as she slipped it in, then fastening it securely again. Finn settled into one corner of his cage and tucked into the porridge while the rest of the family nattered at the table. Hubbub and confusion was the order of the day. Conn gathered up his tea and his pipe, left the table silently and settled into his chair by the fire.

‘What’s the matter, Da?’ Katie asked, a frown creasing her forehead.

‘’Tis nothing. ’Tis nothing, daughter of mine. I’m after wanting a little peace and quiet is all. Leave me be. ’Tis nothing,’ he said with a sigh.

Finn looked up from his porridge, caught the glance of Conn, and winked.

'Right, here's the plan, all of you,' said Dinny. 'Surely, someone in the village will know the answer to the riddle. So 'tis clear we should go out into the streets and ask one and all. Then we'll try the answers out on Finn here. However,' he cautioned, 'be careful. Don't let on we have a leprechaun. Just ask like it was some bit of tomfoolery you're about. If we get the right answer we can afford to share the gold with the one who helped us. Go on now, and make your mammy and me proud, my fine clever lads and lasses. Ask one and all, everyone you meet. We have all of today and till noon tomorrow. That makes nearly two full days. Then a great fortune will be ours.'

'Wait, wait, Dinny. If we divide up the village and countryside, we can reach more people,' suggested Katie. 'That way we won't be wastin' the precious time we've got. I'll pack a ploughman's lunch of bread and cheese for each of you. You can stay out until the sun sets. Write the answers down, loves. We'll try them out on our little friend here at suppertime.'

'Friend, indeed,' grumbled Finn, rattling the wooden slats of his cage.

''Twas my lucky day for sure, the day I married you,' marvelled Dinny. 'You have the best idea. Boys, you go by the Galway road into the village. Rosaleen, take your sister, and cover the back bay road. I'll be goin' first to the landlord, and then down Main Street. Katie, you go to the priest. He's sure to have a good answer for us. Then ask the nuns at the school. Surely one of them knows what is greater than God and more evil than the devil.'

'Conn, will you be helpin' us out?' asked Dinny.

'I'll have no part of this I told you. 'Tis best you be content with what you have. Pining over a fortune that doesn't belong to you can only bring misery down on this house. Count your blessings, son, count your blessings. I'll stay here with Finn and keep the lad company. Sure and have you had any thought at all, at all, for his needs and comfort?'

Conn turned his face away and sighed again, a long drawn out sigh. He caught the eye of Finn, saw the twinkle there, and chuckled to himself.

So it was that, as the village began its daily hustle and bustle, the family of Dinny and Katie darlin' O'Shaughnessy spread out far and wide to search for the answer to the leprechaun's riddle.

The cottage seemed empty and quiet as Conn Donnahey got up to make himself another cup of tea.

'Would you be wantin' another cuppa, leprechaun?' he asked, arranging the kettle over the fire.

'I'd be wantin' out of here, old man. I can tell you're on my side. Let me go. I'll leave ye in peace, and leave a gold coin to boot. I know ye know the answer to the riddle. Why haven't ye told your girl? Ye must be wantin' to let me out of here,' reasoned Finn.

'Sure, and I know the answer as well as you do.' Conn answered. ''Twas one of the first things they taught us in catechism class. It fits the whole riddle. Greed is cloudin' the minds of me darlin' Katie and her family. They all know the answer, but just can't see it yet.

'But I'll not be lettin' you go, Finn, boyo. I can't stand in their way. They would never forgive me, and more: this is a lesson they need to learn for themselves, the lot of them. Settle down now. Leave me some peace, uneasy though it may be.'

Meanwhile, Dinny, with a light skip to his step, reached the manor house behind their farm. As he approached the main gate, Lord Sheamus Burke, owner of most of the farms around Castlebar, came around the side of the house. He reined in his horse when he saw Dinny.

'What can I be helping you with, O'Shaughnessy?' he boomed. 'What brings you up to the manor this fine morning?'

''Tis only that I'm needin' a bit of wisdom, your lordship,' said Dinny. 'Me wife has locked me out of the cottage until I can answer a certain riddle. She says we learned it in school. Since you're the wisest man in these parts, I thought if I put it to you, you would have the answer.'

'Put it to me then, man,' said Lord Burke. 'There's work to be done this day. I've little time to dawdle with riddles. You must have made your Kate very angry indeed.'

'Right, so,' said Dinny, 'here 'tis: What is greater than God and more evil than the devil? The poor have it. The rich need it. If ye eat it, ye will die. What is it?'

A roar came out of the mouth of Lord Burke. 'How dare you bother me with nonsense like this? Be off with you. I've work to do.'

'Sure, what is it, sir? You said you would help me. What makes you so angry?' puzzled Dinny.

'I'll have nothing to do with this idiocy. Nothing!' growled the nobleman, slapping his horse smartly and making off for the fields.

Somewhat put out by the anger of the landlord, Dinny set off toward the main street of the village. Along the way, he encountered Mad Maura Connolly, setting her wash out to dry on some blackberry hedges. As there is a fine line between wisdom and madness, Dinny resolved to ask for her help.

'Maura, me wife is after locking me out of the house until I can answer this riddle. Will you be helpin' me, woman?' Dinny called out.

Mad Maura fixed him with a beady eye. 'You must have been drunk as a skunk, Dinny, for your Katie darlin' to lock you out. What's the riddle?' she said.

'What is greater than God and more evil than the devil? The poor have it. The rich need it. If ye eat it ye will die.'

Mad Maura broke into her usual rasping cackle. 'Sure, everyone knows the answer to that one, Dinny O'Shaughnessy. I'll not be tellin' you, though. I'm on Katie's side.'

'I'm pleadin' with you, Maura,' said Dinny. 'Have pity on a poor homeless man like meself.'

'Hah,' responded Maura, still chuckling. 'You'll be getting nothing out of me today, lad. Nothing.'

'You don't know, do you, woman?' spluttered Dinny, walking away in disgust. 'I'm off. The boys in the pub will help me out. I can count on them.'

While Dinny made his way down the boreen towards the Shamrock Arms, Katie darlin' was a-knocking on the door of the priest's house.

A throaty voice boomed from inside the rectory, 'Who is it that's disturbing my morning prayers?' The door opened slowly and the massive form of Father Shanahan appeared, prayer beads in one hand and a scowl etched across his stern face.

'Ah, Katie,' he said in a softer tone, when he saw the worried look on Katie's face. 'What is it you want, woman? Come in, come in.'

Giving a quick curtsy, Katie followed the priest into his study.

'Sit you down there now. Tell me what's troubling you. I can get back to my prayers later,' said the priest kindly.

'It's like this, your reverence: I need the answer to a riddle in order to make peace in me household. There is so much hubbub going on. Each of me family members think themselves to be smarter than all the others.

There is arguin' and commotion all the long day. I said to meself, Father Shanahan is the smartest man in the village. He'll have the answer. Then we can settle down, and have some quiet again. Do you think you can help me out, Father?'

Katie looked away. She wasn't sure if she had lied to the priest or not. She did know, however, that she had only told him a small part of the truth.

The priest looked at her in a puzzled way. 'Out with it then, girleen,' he said, 'I'll help you if I can.'

'What is greater than God and more evil than the devil? The poor have it. The rich need it. If ye eat it ye will die.'

The priest raised himself up to his full height and hovered over a somewhat frightened Katie.

In his most bombastic voice he hollered, 'What can be greater than God? What can be more evil than the devil? Leave off these subjects and tend to your home and family. Away with you! Don't bother me with the likes of this again. I'm a man of God, with more important things on my mind. Nothing good can come of such frivolity. Nothing!'

Katie darlin' O'Shaughnessy needed no further word from the priest. She picked herself up, took herself off, and ran the rest of the way into the village.

Chapter 5:
THE LONG EVENING

Ribbons of red and gold striped the hillsides, blessing the oncoming twilight, as the weary family members made their separate ways back to the cottage. Conn and Finn, the leprechaun shoemaker, were waiting as, one by one, Katie, Rosaleen, Mary Kate, Michael, Shamie, Jeremiah and, finally, a somewhat tipsy Dinny, came home for their tea.

'I've a meal ready for you, lads and lasses,' said Conn. ''Tis many a long year since I have spent the whole day at home with nothin' to do.

There's a pot of ham, cabbage, and taties boilin' on the hob. Have your tea. Then we'll talk about the day just spent.'

As they partook of the simple fare that Conn had readied for them, the family was quiet and subdued, weary from a long day's walking the highways and byways. Finn, too, was thoughtful and unusually silent, as he ate his portion.

''Tis time for answers now, family of mine,' said Dinny, after the table had been cleared and all had settled with a mug of tea at their place. 'What manner of luck have you had? I'm hopin' it was better than mine.'

'Mrs McGinty chased me off her property with a broom, Da,' answered Jeremiah. 'The only other person who would give me the time of day was Meggie Murphy, the baker. She just laughed at me and gave me a scone.'

'I've had no luck either,' said Shamie. 'Mike took one side of the Galway road and I the other. I knocked on every door. Not a soul would even listen to me.'

'Michael, lad, what say you? Have you any answers for me?' asked Dinny.

'Da,' answered Michael, 'I was havin' no luck at all, and was ready to call it a day, when I reached the greengrocer. I went in and chatted with the cronies who were warmin' themselves around the pot stove, and sippin' tea. They made quite a sport of me and the riddle, but I got some suggestions. Here's the paper. Try them out.'

Dinny squinted at the paper and handed it to Katie darlin'. "Twas your idea, darlin'. You try them out. Don't forget to say, "My answer is ..."'

Taking the paper from Dinny, Katie sat herself down near Finn's little cage.

'My answer is ... the sun,' she said, in a hesitant manner.

Finn rolled around on the floor of his cell, holding his sides and laughing out loud. 'How could the poor be after havin' the sun? Why would the rich be needin' it? And, mind you, how could you be eatin' it?'

Again, she tried. 'My answer is ... Ireland itself, then?'

'Woman,' answered Finn. 'Would ye ever ask yourself the questions of the riddle before ye try them out on me? I'm getting' a stitch in me side from laughin'. 'Tis not Ireland, as ye could plainly see if ye went over the questions first! Ye're tryin' me patience sorely.'

Katie looked hard at Finn. 'A "yes" or a "no" would do nicely, if you please, and we can make short work of this,' she told him.

'My answer is ... diamonds,' tried Katie, this time just from off the top of her head.

'No!' boomed Finn.

Dinny beckoned Katie to a corner of the kitchen.

'We're not doing too well, a stór. Let's see if the girls fared better.' Turning to the family once again, he nodded to his daughters and asked, 'Rosaleen and Mary Kate, did you find anyone to help us out?'

Rosaleen spoke up. 'We stopped and talked to the fishermen along the back bay, and on the wharf. We came up with one possible answer. Mary Kate ran into Jacko, the tinker, in his donkey cart. He made a suggestion too. Here.' She handed her father a piece of paper.

'Your turn to try, Dinny,' said Katie. 'I'm tired of being made fun of by that spit of a thing.'

Dinny paced around the outside of the pen. Finn regarded him with a triumphant air. 'Well?' he bellowed. 'Out with it.'

'My answer is ... gold. Now, why didn't I think of that?' pondered a perplexed Dinny, looking at the paper Rosaleen had given him.

'Guess again,' answered Finn.

'My answer is ... hope,' tried Dinny.

'Aye, 'tis a good try, the best one yet,' replied Finn, in a wry manner. 'But think for a minute, ye dumb ox. Is hope greater than God? Is hope more evil than the devil? Most of all, can ye be after eatin' hope?'

'What about you, Katie? Did Father Shanahan or the holy sisters give you any suggestions?' Dinny asked.

Katie shook her head sadly. 'They told me nothin'. And you, Dinny, how did you fare?'

'Sure, everyone I asked thought I was just botherin' them over nothin'. They seemed to think I was askin' a foolish question. The boys in the pub just laughed. "Nothin' doin'," they said, and went back to their pints.'

Conn looked up from his pipe at his disappointed daughter and frustrated son-in-law. 'Give it a rest now, family. You can try again in the mornin'. Sleep on it. Perhaps the answer will come when you're least expectin' it.' He stood up, stretched and ushered the children to their beds.

A silence descended over the house. Night sounds and occasional creaks were all that could be heard as the long day ended. Katie and Dinny sat over the dregs of their tea, and poured out their disappointment to each other.

As they moaned and groaned, an idea began to take shape in the mind of Katie darlin'. Her eyes lit up.

'Dinny,' she said. 'The dictionary! The dictionary I won as a prize for bein' the best speller. Let's try that out. We have all night. We can try every word. Perhaps if we wear Finn out, he'll be droppin' us a hint.'

Reaching into the cabinet that held the few treasures the family possessed, Katie pulled out her dog-eared copy of the Complete Collected Dictionary of English. Together, they pulled up a bench in front of Finn's cage, and began.

'My answer is ... aardvark,' suggested Katie.

'No.'

'My answer is ... aardwolf,' tried Dinny.

'No. Ye're not really goin' to do this, are ye?' asked Finn. 'Only, I'll be needin' me sleep.

Tomorrow is a big day for me. I'll be free. Ye won't catch me in this county again.'

Page by page, Katie and Dinny took turns trying each and every word. After a couple of hours of this, they could barely keep their eyes open. Finn, too, was beginning to nod his head with fatigue.

'My answer is ... gab,' said Katie, as she began on the letter 'G' words.

'Let me know when you get to the ...' Finn stopped mid-breath. He had almost given it away.

Katie, ears alert, was crestfallen when Finn did not finish the sentence. She shook Dinny, who had fallen asleep, his head resting on her shoulder. 'Come on Dinny, it will be dawn soon. We've done our best today. After some rest we can start fresh.'

She turned to Finn and put the towel over

his cage. 'Sleep well, leprechaun,' she said, but he had already curled up and nodded off.

As the darkness faded into light, Katie, still wakeful, turned to her husband.

'Dinny,' she said. 'I haven't slept a wink. We've only a few hours left. I don't think we'll come up with the answer, do you?'

'No darlin', I don't think we will. And do you know what? I'm thinkin' we should let the little fella go. What say you?' answered Dinny. Katie sat bolt upright in the bed, surprised at her husband's change of mind, yet happy that he realized what had been in her heart all along.

'Sure, what would we be doin' with a pot of gold anyway?' Katie darlin' asked. 'We have all we'll ever need right here, a ghrá. We have each other, our children and a good home, as well as good friends and neighbours.

What could we buy that would be better than what we already have?'

'You're right, Katie. This house and these fields will be ours one day. Your da told me on our weddin' day that one day I'd have the lot. We'll always be taken care of. Let's do it.'

Chapter 6:
Real Treasure

Conn Donnahey was up, with the fire lit and the kettle set to boiling, when Katie and Dinny came into the kitchen.

'Daddy-o,' said Katie, 'Dinny and I have something to say.'

'What is it, daughter?' asked Conn.

'Join us at the table and we'll tell you,' answered Katie.

Finn looked sideways through narrowed eyes at Dinny and Katie. 'Time is wastin', you two. 'Tis a free leprechaun I am by noon this day.'

'Conn,' said Dinny, turning to his father-in-law, 'we're of a mind to let Finn go. 'Tis a fact that we've tried our best and cannot answer the riddle. We talked it up and down in the small hours of this mornin' and, well, we think 'tis best.'

'Da,' put in Katie darlin', 'the long and short of it is that we have all we need right here. What would we be doin' with a pot of gold, except spendin' the rest of our lives hoardin' and protectin' it, and worryin' about it? You and the children are our real treasure.'

A smile spread out over Conn's face. 'I think you're right, daughter. Let him go now, before the village wakes. He'll have a better chance to make a clean getaway.'

Finn could scarce believe his ears. They were letting him go!

'Well, leprechaun, you've won. We have no need of your gold,' said Dinny, as he lifted the bar on the pen. 'Now leave us before I change me mind.'

Finn didn't need telling twice. He bolted for the door as soon as Dinny opened the cage.

'Wait!' yelled Katie, as he was about to slip out of their lives forever. 'The answer. Now that you have your freedom, tell us the answer to the riddle. You've exhausted us with the effort of tryin' to find out.'

Finn put his hands on his hips and sneered, 'I'm tellin' you nothin'! Nothin', mind you! Nothin'!'

With these last words, Finn grabbed his shoemaking tools and was out through the door and gone quicker than you could blink an eye.

'We'll never know then,' said Dinny. 'What a waste of two days.'

'I know the answer,' said Conn Donnahey. 'You know the answer too, if you would but look in your heart. It's been right before you all along. You were too blinded with greed to see it.'

'What is greater than God, loves? Nothin'. What is more evil than the devil? Nothin'. What do the poor have? Nothin'. What do the rich need? Nothin'. And if ye eat nothin', ye will die. That's the answer – nothin'. I'm sure you knew it all along,' Conn told them.

Dinny looked at Katie. Katie looked at Dinny. Taking Conn's hands, they danced a merry jig around the empty pen. The laugh started from deep down inside of them, rose up and bubbled out in a merry peal. The sound of it woke the children from their beds, and they rushed into the kitchen and joined in, until the whole family was dancing in a circle around the room.

Conn, breathless and laughing, pulled away and said with a wink, 'Sure you made the right decision, the two of you. Nothin' could make me happier, nothin'!'

GLOSSARY

a ghrá – my love (pronounced 'a graw').

a stór – my dear (pronounced 'a store').

boreen – a small, narrow country road or lane.

catechism – a short book, in question-and-answer form, outlining the basic principles of a religion.

cuppa – a cup of a beverage, usually tea.

Da – Daddy.

Daddy-o – another way of referring to Daddy.

dropsy – a disease that is characterised by the retention of too much bodily fluid.

girleen – little girl.

hob – a shelf or projection inside a fireplace or on top of a stove, used to keep food or water warm.

scone – a small, biscuit-like pastry or quickbread.

stirabout – another name for oatmeal or porridge.

nattering – talking a lot or chattering idly.

smithy – a blacksmith.

tinker – a travelling mender of metal objects, such as pots and pans.

tomfoolery – trivial or foolish behaviour; nonsense.

tucked into – began to eat with great enthusiasm.